We Love You to the Moon

Colton

By Suzanne Marshall

LiveWellMedia.com

ISBN: 9798860807518

We Love You to the Moon, Colton

Suzanne Marshall

This book is dedicated to

Colton

who is loved very much!

~ *Colton* ~

even if you were an owl

ready for sleep,

we'd still love you from

your wings to your beak.

~ *Colton* ~

even if you were an elephant

napping at dusk,

we'd still love you from

your trunk to your tusks.

~ *Colton* ~

even if you were a koala
sleeping like a log,
we'd still love you from
your head to your paws.

~ Colton ~

even if you were a giraffe

as tall as can be,

we'd still love you easily.

(We'd kiss you from a ladder or tree.)

~ *Colton* ~

even if you were a bear

snoring loudly,

we'd still love you

very proudly.

~ *Colton* ~

even if you were a bee

and really quite small,

we'd still love you

buzzing and all.

~ *Colton* ~

even if you were a lion

with a furry mane,

we'd still love you

in sunshine and rain.

~ *Colton* ~

even if you were a bat

with a tiny snout,

we'd still love you

inside and out.

~ *Colton* ~

even if you were a polar bear

as white as snow,

we'd still love you

wherever you go.

~ Colton ~

even if you were a panda
resting on a limb,
we'd still love you
through thick and thin.

~ *Colton* ~

even if you were a kitty

sleeping sweetly,

we'd still love you

very deeply.

~ *Colton* ~

even if you were a tiger

with a lot of stripes,

we'd still love you

morning, day and night.

~ *Colton* ~

even if you were a puppy

dozing away,

we'd still love you

forever and a day.

~ *Colton* ~

even if you were a bunny

who hops a lot,

we'd still love you

no matter what.

As you sleep, Colton,

remember that:

We love you to the moon and back.

(Pictured above: Suzanne Marshall and Abby Underdog)

About the Author

Suzanne Marshall writes to inspire, engage and empower children. Her books are full of affirmations, inspiration and unconditional love. An honors graduate of Smith College, Suzanne has made it her misson to spread love through storytelling. Learn more at **LiveWellMedia.com**.

Credits

All illustrations were edited by the author. Moon/stars were curated @ freepik; clouds @ medialoot; animals @ fotosearch.com: Bat, Bear, Bee, Bunny, Elephant, Lion, Owl & Panda: © Tigatelu. Kitty, Polar Bear, Puppy, Tiger, Mouse: © Dazdraperma. Giraffe & Koala: © colematt.

Made in the USA
Las Vegas, NV
15 September 2024